Angelica watched openmouthed as the pinecone sailed over Susie's head and through the open window. *Bonk!* It hit the teacher's quill pen out of his hand!

"Uh-oh!" said Angelica. She looked around wildly. If there was one thing she learned in nursery school, it was that throwing things at teachers was bad! It was time for a quick decision. Someone was about to get in big trouble.

Well, it isn't gonna be Angelica Pickles, she thought. And then she ran like the wind.

Rugrats Chapter Books

Star-Spangled Babies

ISBN 0-439-16511-3

12 11 10 9 8 7 6 5 4 3 2   2 3 4 5/0

Printed in the U.S.A.

First Scholastic printing, January 2000

Star-Spangled Babies

by Kitty Richards
illustrated by Jose Maria Cardona

Scholastic Inc.
New York Toronto London Auckland Sydney
Mexico City New Delhi Hong Kong

Chapter 1

"Guess what I gots in my pocket?" Susie Carmichael asked with a grin. Susie was Tommy Pickles's neighbor. She was in Tommy's backyard with Angelica and the babies. Grandpa Lou was dozing nearby.

"A present for me?" asked Angelica.

"Nope," Susie said.

"Oh," said Angelica, turning back to her doll. "Do you feel like being a supermodel today, Cynthia?" she asked. "Or maybe a president?"

"Susie, do you have a slug?" guessed

Phil. He and his twin sister, Lil, loved bugs and anything else that squished, slimed, or went *splat*.

Susie shook her head.

"A *dead* slug?" asked Lil.

"A peeny butter sandwich?" suggested Tommy.

"Uh-uh," said Susie.

Chuckie took a guess. "A flower?"

Again Susie shook her head. "You're all wrong. What I gots in my pocket is . . ." she paused, then whispered, "my 'lowance."

Angelica raised her eyebrows but pretended not to be impressed. "Big deal," she said with a shrug.

"Oooooh," gasped Phil, Lil, Chuckie, and Tommy. Then they looked at each other.

"What's a 'lowance?" Tommy asked.

"It's what you get from your mom and dad every week for helpin' out,"

9

Susie explained to the babies.

"No, no, no," said Angelica. "You gots it all wrong. A 'lowance is what you get from your dad for not screaming in the soupymarket."

"Well, let's see it," said Phil.

Susie reached into her pocket and pulled out a crisp dollar bill. The kids crowded around. Even Angelica came over for a peek.

"What's it for?" Tommy asked.

"You can buy stuff with it," said Susie.

"Who's the guy with the white hair?" asked Lil.

"It's the fried chicken guy," said Angelica. "But that's not what a 'lowance is supposed to look like. Mine always has a guy with a beard on it. His name is Honest Babe." Angelica narrowed her eyes and looked at Susie. "Hey, Carmichael, I'll give ya *two* Honest Babes for that *one* chicken-guy dollar!"

Susie shook her head. "No thanks, Angelica. 'Sides, I think it's a Georgie Washingmachine dollar," she said.

"Darn tootin' it's George Washington," said Grandpa Lou. He had woken up and was turning the pages of his newspaper. "You sprouts don't know much about history, do you?"

The kids looked at him blankly.

"In my day we loved history," Grandpa continued. "Couldn't get enough of it. Why, I'd walk *fifteen* miles in a snowstorm to borrow a history book."

Just then Didi, Tommy's mom, came downstairs holding Tommy's little brother Dil. "Thanks for watching the kids, Pop," she said. "Stu is just so excited to go to this Baby Inventions Fair!"

Stu stuck his head out of the kitchen. "I can't wait to see the strides they've made in musical potties," he said.

Suddenly Grandpa spotted something

in the newspaper. "Hey!" he said. "Today on the Nothing-but-History Channel is the 'That's America! Marathon.' All day long nothing but presidents, treaties, and doctrines. Me and the kids will watch it. By the time it's over, they'll be reciting the Constitution backwards and forwards."

"The Constipation?" Lil said softly. "That doesn't sound so good."

Didi wrinkled her brow. "Well, we don't want to put any unnecessary pressure on the children," she said. "But I've heard Dr. Lipschitz say many times, 'Ze children are never too young to learn about ze history.'"

"Sounds like a great idea, Pop," said Stu. "See you later!"

Didi gave Tommy a big kiss, and the three were on their way.

"A whole afternoon of history," said Grandpa Lou happily.

Angelica turned to the kids, with her hands on her hips. "This is just great! Now we gots to watch boring old eddy-cational TV all day," she groaned. "If you hadn't shown us your 'lowance, Susie Carmichael, this never would have happened." She glared at Susie. "It's all your fault!"

Chapter 2

"Five minutes to show time," said Grandpa Lou. "I can't tell you sprouts just how lucky you are. The history you'll see unfold before your young eyes today—the Mayflower Compact! The Declaration of Independence! The French and Indian War!"

"The war!" Chuckie whispered. "I don't like the sound of this!"

"Don't worry, Chuckie," said Tommy. "It's just TB."

Grandpa Lou checked his watch. "It's time," he said. He switched on the TV

with a flourish. Patriotic music swelled.

Chuckie cocked his head. "I think I heard this song afore," he said.

"It's the 'Star-Spangled Banana,' silly," Angelica said.

The kids settled onto the couch as a map of the United States appeared on the screen. A familiar-looking man stepped up to the camera.

"Hello, and welcome to the 'That's America! Marathon,'" he said. "I am your host, Rex Pester. The year is 1492. A man named Christopher Columbus stares out at the empty sea. He dreams of reaching China by a direct sea route. . . ."

But before the *Niña*, the *Pinta*, or the *Santa Maria* had even set sail, Grandpa Lou was sound asleep in his La-Z-Boy.

Angelica, Susie, and the babies saw the exploration of the New World.

After a while, the *Mayflower* was launched. Then colonial America came to life on the small screen.

Zzzzzz, snored Grandpa Lou.

Chapter 3

The strains of "Yankee Doodle Dandy" stirred Grandpa Lou out of his sleep. "Hey, that's my favorite historical era!" he said. He pointed to the white-haired man on the TV screen. "That's George Washington," said Grandpa Lou. "People call him the 'father of our country.' He was the first president of the United States of America—and he's the guy on Susie's dollar bill!"

Soon Grandpa Lou's eyes started getting heavier again. By the time Washington crossed the Delaware River, he was back in Dreamland

"I'm bored," announced Angelica. "Let's go outside and play." She marched toward the backyard, then glanced over her shoulder. "You babies with me, or what?" She looked slyly at Phil and Lil. "There's lotsa bugs out there, ya know."

Immediately the twins were up and running. Susie looked at Tommy and Chuckie. "C'mon, guys, we'll be back before the show's over," she said.

"Okay," said Tommy.

Chuckie sighed. "I guess I hafta go too."

Together the kids slid open the door to the backyard. They stood blinking in the bright afternoon sunlight and looked out at an open field. Cows grazed on the hillside. Birds sang and butterflies fluttered. A small white building with a big bell on top was nearby. Tommy looked around curiously as the grass tickled his

feet. There was something different about his backyard.

Phil pried a big, heavy rock off the ground. "Look, Lil, worms!" he shouted.

"Wow!" she exclaimed. "That one has a hunnert legs!"

"It's called a millionpede," her twin added wisely.

Susie and Angelica took off in opposite directions chasing butterflies.

"Tommy," said Chuckie, "I don't remember no cows in your backyard!"

"Me either!" said Tommy. "Isn't this great?"

Susie's butterfly took her closer and closer to the white building. She stopped chasing the butterfly and peeked in through a window. Then she waved to Tommy and Chuckie to join her.

The two boys toddled over.

"What is it, Susie?" Tommy asked.

"Look in the window!" said Susie.

"There's all these boys wearin' funny clothes."

Tommy stood on the tips of his toes to take a look. The room was full of boys wearing jackets, white shirts, short pants, white stockings, and shoes with buckles. They were sitting on wooden benches and writing with quill pens. A man stood at the front of the room. He had a white powdered wig on his head.

"Hey, guys," said Phil, running up to them. "Whatcha lookin' at?"

"I think it's a school," said Susie. "'Cept there aren't any girls."

Angelica sauntered over and pushed Chuckie out of the way. "Let me see," she said as she stuck her face at the window. "If it's a school, where's the doll corner? Where's the play kitchen?"

"Let me see too!" said Lil. She and Phil jockeyed for position at the window.

"I need more room, Lillian," said Phil.

"Your head is too big, Philip," said Lil.

"You're in my way, Susie," whined Angelica.

"Who lied and made you boss?" said Susie.

Angelica stared at Susie, then stomped off to pout beneath a tall fir tree. "Ow!" she said as she sat down. She reached under and pulled out something small and round and hard. "Dumb pinecomb!"

Angelica tossed the pinecone . . . and it flew toward Susie!

"Oops!" said Angelica. Hearing Angelica, Susie turned around and ducked just in time. Angelica watched openmouthed as the pinecone sailed over Susie's head and through the open window. *Bonk!* It hit the teacher's quill pen out of his hand!

"Uh-oh!" said Angelica. She looked around wildly. If there was one thing she learned in nursery school, it was that throwing things at teachers was bad! It was time for a quick decision. Someone was about to get in big trouble.

Well, it isn't gonna be Angelica Pickles, she thought. And then she ran like the wind.

Chapter 4

Chuckie watched Angelica take off. "Boy, she runs fast," he said admiringly.

Phil and Lil went to hunt for bugs. Susie and the babies stayed at the window and watched the teacher walk over to a small boy with a brown ponytail seated in the last row. The teacher grabbed the boy by the arm, marched him to a corner, and put a pointy hat on his head.

"Oh!" said Tommy. "It must be that little boy's burp-day!"

Susie nodded. "And, look, it says

something on his hat," she said. "It must be his name!"

"If it's his burp-day, that means there's gonna be a party with balloonies and I scream cake," Tommy said. "Maybe he'll invite us."

At last the school bell rang, and all the kids spilled out of the schoolhouse. All except the boy with the pointy hat, who still sat in the corner. After what seemed like a long time, the teacher walked the boy outside and then headed back in. The little boy sat down on the steps and sighed.

As soon as the teacher shut the schoolroom door, Tommy, Chuckie, and Susie ran over.

"Hi," said Susie. "Happy burp-day!"

"Are you havin' a party?" asked Tommy.

"With balloonies and presents and cake?" asked Chuckie.

The boy looked bewildered. "You must be mistaken. It is not the day of my birth. That is not until February twenty-second."

"But you were wearin' a burp-day hat!" Tommy said.

The boy blushed, then laughed sheepishly. "The pointed hat I was made to wear is a dunce cap. I had to wear it because my schoolmaster thinks I was bad. And he told me I cannot return to school until I apologize for throwing that pinecone. But I did not do it!" He shook his head. "I *must* do something to make my schoolmaster believe me."

"We believe you," said Tommy.

"'Cause we saw Angelica do it!" said Susie.

"Really?" said the boy.

Susie and the babies nodded.

"Can you please help me find this Angelica?" the boy asked.

"Sure!" said Tommy.

"But I do not even know your names!" said the boy.

"I'm Susie Carmichael," Susie said. "The twins digging in the dirt over there are Phil and Lil. And this is Tommy Pickles and Chuckie Finster."

"Pleased to make your acquaintance," said the boy. "My name is George Washington."

Chapter 5

"Georgie Washyton!" cried Tommy. "We just saw Georgie Washyton on telly-vision!"

"I know not of this telly-vision you speak of," said George. "How did you chance to see me upon it?"

"Grandpa Lou made us watch," explained Tommy. "And Georgie Washyton was on it." He gave George a skeptical glance. "And he looked a lot biggerer than you!"

"Yeah!" said Phil and Lil together. They had abandoned their bug hunt and joined the group.

"But I *am* George Washington," the boy insisted. "And I *never* tell a lie."

"Excuse us for a moment, Georgie," said Susie. She pulled the babies aside.

"It can't be him; he's too little!" Tommy insisted.

"I thought Georgie Washyton was the *father* of our country," said Phil.

"I never seen a daddy that little afore," said Chuckie.

"Yeah, but if he wears a white wig . . ." said Susie. She thought for a moment. "I know! He's on my 'lowance all growed up. We can see if it looks like him." She took out her dollar bill.

"Oh, my Bob!" she cried out.

"What's wrong?" said Lil.

"Georgie Washyton isn't on my 'lowance," she said. "It's a lady with a crown instead!"

"What does that mean?" said Tommy.

"I dunno," said Susie. "Anyway, Georgie Washyton's an important guy. Kids always get off school on his burp-day. So we gots to help him."

Susie and the babies told George what had happened: how Angelica had thrown the pinecone that had hit the teacher's pen by accident. And how she had run away.

George scratched his head. "But why would she run away?" he asked. "Why would she let me get into trouble for something she did?"

"Angelica was borned that way," said Tommy. "But we'll find her and make her tell your teacher the truth. We gots to do it for the 'Nited Skates of 'Merica."

George stared at them. "The *what?*" he asked.

Chapter 6

Meanwhile Angelica was making pretty good time getting as far away from the schoolhouse as she could. She ran through the field. She zoomed past the cow pasture. She dashed over a bridge. She wasn't exactly sure where she was going, but she kept on running.

Soon she arrived at a small village. Whew! She was winded. She stopped to catch her breath.

What a weird place this was! There were no cars, no telephone poles, no mail boxes. Angelica stared in amazement as a herd of pigs trotted down the street, pausing to snuffle around in the mud. A horse and wagon rattled by. She stared at the muddy street in disgust. Yuck!

"I'm thirsty," she said. She knew there had to be a soda machine around there somewhere. Reaching into her pocket, she pulled out a few coins. Maybe after she had a nice cold Reptar Cola, things would start to make more sense.

There were no soda machines on the block she was on, so she rounded a corner. A boy whose face was buried in a book bumped right into her.

Cynthia—and the change—fell out of Angelica's hands and onto the muddy street. "Hey!" Angelica cried. "Watch where you're going!"

"Begging your pardon, ma'am," said the boy. He was short, a little chubby, and had long brown hair. A small pair of

wire-rimmed glasses were perched on his nose. Angelica fished her soiled Cynthia out of the muck and glared at him.

"Pleased to make your acquaintance," said the boy. "Benjamin Franklin, at your service."

"Save it, Ben," said Angelica. "Just help me pick up my monies."

Ben knelt down and picked up the coins, wiping them off carefully with a white handkerchief before handing them back to her.

"A penny saved is a penny burned," said Ben wisely. Then he frowned. "Or maybe it's 'churned.' Or could it be 'spurned'?"

"That's just dumb," said Angelica. "Now what are you gonna do 'bout my Cynthia? Her pretty dress is ripped. And it's dirty, too!"

"Well, you could take it to Betsy's

house. She loves to sew. Maybe she could fix it for you." He pointed to a small, cheery-looking cottage at the end of the lane. "That's the house," he said.

"All-righty," said Angelica as she headed off. "And next time don't walk and read at the same time!"

"Wait!" called Ben. "Always remember that a stitch in time saves pine!" He paused. "Or does it save 'mine'? Or perhaps 'wine'?"

"Oh, go fly a kite!" Angelica yelled back.

"Hmm," Ben said. He watched thoughtfully as Angelica made her way across the muddy street and down the lane. "What an excellent idea! I might just try that!"

"How far is it?" Phil whined. It was almost his naptime, and he was getting a little cranky.

"Just a mile or so," said George.

Phil groaned. They had walked through the field, past the cow pasture, across the bridge, and into the town.

"Where are the cars?" said Susie.

"The what?" replied George.

"What's that?" asked Chuckie, pointing to a strange-looking wooden contraption that stood in the middle of the town square. There was a small seat, and in front of it was a piece of wood with two holes in it.

"That's the stocks," said George solemnly. "That's where bad people go. And sometimes people throw vegetables at them when they're locked in there."

"Oh," said Chuckie. That sounded scary!

"Hello, George!" someone called.

George turned around. "Hello, Ben!" he called back.

Ben closed his book and walked

toward them. "You got into a bit of trouble today at school, didn't you?"

George hung his head. "But my new friends are going to help me find the girl who did it, and clear my name," he said.

"That's wonderful!" said Ben. "You had better hurry because the early bird catches the germ!" Then he shook his head. "No, that's not right. . . ."

The kids looked puzzled.

"Oh, don't mind Ben," said George. "He's always coming up with things like that. Someday he's going to write a book of sayings."

"I wonder if the girl I met today is the one you are looking for," Ben said.

"What did she look like?" asked Tommy.

"She had yellow hair and a most unpleasant disposition," said Ben.

"Huh?" said the babies.

"He means she wasn't very nice,"

40

George explained to the babies.

"That's Angelica!" said Tommy. "Which way did she go?"

"I sent her to Betsy's house," said Ben. "She wanted someone to fix her doll's dress."

"Thank you, Ben," Susie said. "You've been very helpful!"

Ben smiled. "You're quite welcome," he said.

"Forward, Marge!" shouted Lil.

"Forward, Marge!" repeated George. "I like the sound of that!" he said.

Chapter 7

When Angelica reached the end of the lane, she found herself in front of a small, ivy-covered cottage. There was a vegetable garden in the side yard, and a huge oak tree in the front. A girl in a long dress who had curly brown hair was sitting in the shade of the tree, sewing.

She smiled at Angelica.

"Hey!" said Angelica. "Is your name Betsy?"

"Why, yes it is," said the girl pleasantly, standing up and smoothing her skirt. "Betsy Ross. How can I help you?"

Angelica showed her Cynthia's torn dress. "Some kid with glasses told me you could fix it," she said.

"Let me see," said Betsy, taking a good look at the tear. "Oh, this should be easy," she said. "But it is a little dirty. We should wash it first." She took off Cynthia's muddy dress. "What an odd doll," she said. "What is she made of?"

"Oh, plastic, I guess," said Angelica.

Betsy shrugged. "Plastic . . . it must be a new kind of wood," she said. She rinsed the dress at the water pump.

"We'll just wait for the dress to dry, and then I'll fix it," said Betsy, laying the dress on the grass. "Now let me show you what I've made," she added. "Do you like this striped petticoat?"

Angelica nodded. It was very nice.

"How about this cap with stars on it?" Betsy said. "I think it is quite fetching."

"Very, uh, fetching, I guess," said Angelica. "Is Cynthia's dress dry yet?"

☆   ☆   ☆

At last the dress was dry, and Betsy had repaired it.

"Thank you very much," said Angelica. "You are a really good sewer!"

"The pleasure was mine," Betsy said. Then she peered down the lane. "My goodness, what a busy afternoon I am having!" she said. "Here comes my friend George." She shook her head. "I hear poor George got in trouble at school today. I hope he is not too upset."

Angelica spun around. In trouble? At school? That was her cue to exit, and fast!

"Oops, gotta run!" said Angelica, grabbing Cynthia. "Thanks again! And I really liked the stars and stripes!"

"What an odd girl," Betsy said to herself. "But she liked the stars *and* stripes. . . ."

"Hi, Betsy!" George called when he, Susie, and the babies reached her gate. "Ben told us he sent a girl your way. A girl with yellow hair and a doll she calls Cynthia."

"Why, yes, he did," said Betsy. "As a matter of fact, you just missed her."

"Which way did she go?" asked Susie.

Betsy pointed east. "She headed out behind the house. My guess is that she is going to King George Pond."

Chapter 8

Angelica ran through the woods as fast as she could. That was a close call! She never should have spent so much time at that Betsy girl's house!

"I'll never let 'em catch us, Cynthia," Angelica said.

Rabbits and field mice scampered away as she stomped through the bushes.

Soon she came to a quiet pond. Fish jumped, and frogs splashed onto lily pads. Ducks paddled in the reeds.

On the other side, she saw a boy with

a fishing pole. Maybe he could help her! She ran all the way around the pond.

"Greetings," said the boy. He was eating a picnic lunch as he fished on the sunny bank. He held up a teacup. "Would you care to have tea with me?"

Angelica looked around. But there were no babies in sight, so she said, "Of course!" Tea was only for grown-ups at her house!

The boy had just finished pouring Angelica a steaming cup of tea when George, Susie, and the babies arrived at the other side of the pond.

"There she is!" whispered Tommy.

"She's talking to my friend Sam Adams," said George. "We must sneak up . . . and surprise her!"

"We'll never make it around this pond in time," said Susie.

"Never fear, troops," George said. "I know where a neighbor keeps a boat

hidden in the reeds. We'll be across in no time."

Everyone piled into the boat while Angelica was about to take her first sip of that forbidden grown-up drink. Then, hearing a splash, she looked across the water and saw the babies coming her way.

"Sam! Don't let her get away!" George cried.

"Pardon me," Sam politely told Angelica, "but I will have to ask you to stay right here."

"No such luck, fish boy!" snapped Angelica as she tossed her tea—cup and all—into the pond. Then she ran off.

Samuel Adams stared at the teacup bobbing in the water. "Hmm . . ." he said.

"She's running away!" cried George, standing up and pointing. "Stop her!" he shouted as he stamped his foot.

Suddenly the boat began to sway. "Oh,

no," George cried, losing his balance.

Splash!

"Man overboat!" cried Tommy. Susie reached into the water and pulled George back into the boat. He sat there, sputtering.

"Let that be a lesson to you, Georgie," Susie said as they neared the shore. "No more standing in boats!"

"Whew, that was close," Angelica said to Cynthia. "Those babies almost got me that time."

Maybe now that that Georgie kid is all wet, they'll give up, she thought.

Angelica skipped down a wooded path, chatting away to Cynthia.

"Frankly, I dunno why the grown-ups make such a big deal 'bout tea," she said. "It's yucky! Give me hot chocolate any day!"

She walked until she got to a farm

with a big red barn. "This is the perfect place, Cynthia," she said. "They'll never find us here."

She slipped inside the barn.

"Fancy meeting you here," said a voice.

Angelica found herself face-to-face with a small boy.

"I saw you outside my school today," said the boy. "You're the one who threw the pinecone at the teacher and got George Washington in trouble."

"I dunno what you're talking 'bout," Angelica fibbed.

The boy laughed. "Don't worry. That George is such a Goody Two-shoes. If I hear him say 'I never tell a lie' one more time, I will scream! I am glad he got in trouble."

Angelica smiled. Now things were going her way! She liked this kid.

"I can help you," the boy said.

"Just follow me!"

Angelica followed him out the barn door and into the woods. "Hey, what did you say your name was?" she asked.

"My name is Benedict. Benedict Arnold."

Chapter 9

"I'm tired, Benedict!" said Angelica. "It feels like we've been running around in circles. Are you sure you know where you're going?"

"Of course I do," said Benedict. "We're almost there."

Finally they arrived in the town square. Angelica could hardly lift her feet. "I gots to sit," she said.

"Why don't you sit right here," said Benedict, motioning to the stocks. "There's even a place to rest your feet."

Angelica was pleased. "I think I will,"

she said. She plopped onto the bench and stretched her legs into the notches in the wooden plank.

"Got you!" cried the boy, lowering the top half of the plank and locking it shut.

"Hey . . . what's goin' on here?" Angelica demanded. "Let me out!"

"Now, don't move," Benedict said with a grin. "I'll be back!"

"Oh, Cynthia." Angelica sighed. "What a double-crosser Benedict Arnold turned out to be!"

The kids, all with long faces, walked slowly back into town. George's buckled shoes squished as he walked. His ponytail was a bedraggled mess.

"I give up," said George. "I'll just never go back to school again. I'll become a butcher. Or a baker. Or maybe even a candlestick maker. Who needs school, anyway? Not me!"

Suddenly a voice called, "George! Hey, George!" The kids turned around. It was Ben. "I just ran into Benedict. He said you should meet him in the town square."

"Maybe he has news about Angelica!" said George. "Let's go!"

The kids started to run.

"Slow down!" Ben called after them. "Haste makes paste, you know!"

When the kids reached the town square, they saw that a crowd had gathered around the stocks. The kids made their way to the front. And they saw Angelica, all locked up.

"Let me outta here!" Angelica yelled.

"First you hafta tell the truth, Angelica!" said Tommy.

"Never!" said Angelica.

"But you gots to!" said Chuckie.

"Yeah," said Lil. "George is the brother of our country!"

"You mean the father, Lillian," said Phil.

"No, he's the brother, Philip," said Lil.

"Angelica, it's not fair!" said Tommy. "Tell the truth!"

"No, no, no!" Angelica crossed her arms and looked the other way.

Susie had an idea. "All right," she said. "I guess we'll just have to go. Bye, Angelica."

Angelica's lower lip started to tremble. "You're not going to leave me here, are you?"

"See you later, elevator," said Lil. They began to walk away.

"Oh, all right! *I'm* the one who threw the pinecomb!" Angelica finally admitted.

George smiled. He told Angelica that they would let her go as soon as she told his teacher the truth. But first someone had to get the schoolmaster.

"I'll do it," volunteered a boy. He mounted his pony and rode off in a cloud of dust.

Before long he came galloping back. "The teacher is coming! The teacher is coming!" he shouted.

"That Paul Revere is one fast rider," said George admiringly.

Soon the schoolmaster arrived. He walked up to the stocks.

"Do you have something to say, Angelica?" said Susie.

Angelica muttered under her breath.

"Louder," said Susie.

Angelica glowered. "I said, I'm the one who threw the pinecomb, not George."

The teacher shook his head, then turned to George. "I'm sorry I doubted you, George," he said. "I should have known you'd never tell a lie."

Benedict groaned.

"Hooray!" cried the kids.

58

"Now everything is back to Norman," Tommy said.

George turned to the kids. "I don't know how to thank you."

"It was our treasure," said Tommy. "Give me a high five."

George looked puzzled. "A *high what*?"

"A high five," said Tommy. He and Chuckie raised their hands in the air and slapped palms. "Oh, I see," said George. It took him a couple of tries, but he finally got it right.

"Hello! Can someone *please* let me outta here?" yelled Angelica. "It's not very umfortable!"

"What are you sprouts doing out here?" said a voice. It sounded so familiar . . . it sounded like . . . Grandpa Lou!

"They're just about to sign the Constitution! Hurry!" He went back into the house.

Angelica, Susie, and the babies looked

around. They were in Tommy's backyard! Angelica sat in the sandbox, her legs dangling over the side. "Let me out, let me out—oh, never mind," she said.

Everyone plopped down in front of the TV. And there on the screen was George Washington, all grown up. He picked up a quill pen and signed the Constitution with a flourish. Then he turned to Benjamin Franklin, who stood next to him. They both raised their hands in the air and gave each other a high five.

Susie pulled out her dollar. Sure enough, George Washington's face was on the bill. "Look, you guys," she whispered to the babies. "We did it for the 'Nited Skates of 'Merica!"

About the Author

Kitty Richards is the pseudonym for a children's book editor and writer in New York City. She is the author of over thirty books for children, including the Rugrats titles, *Once Upon a Reptar*, *Ice Cream Fun Day*, and *Hang on to Your Diapies, Babies, We're Going In!* While she has never traveled through time, Kitty once acted as Paul Revere in a play at the Kingsland Homestead in Flushing, Queens. If you ask her nicely, she will be pleased to reenact the "one if by land, two if by sea" scene. But for now, her main audience is her husband and their two cats, Felix and Oscar.